Cat on the Hill

To Valentine, the horse,
Edward, the donkey,
Ted, the dog,
and our cat, Tex

hinkler

Published by Hinkler Books Pty Ltd
45–55 Fairchild Street
Heatherton Victoria 3202 Australia
www.hinklerbooks.com

First published by Andersen Press Ltd., London

Text © Michael Foreman 2003
Illustrations © Michael Foreman 2003
Cover design © Hinkler Books 2010

Cover design: Peter Tovey
Prepress: Graphic Print Group

ISBN: 978 1 7435 2443 5

Printed and bound in China

Cat on the Hill

MICHAEL FOREMAN

hinkler

SUMMER

AAAH! It's good to
be here, under these old stone steps.
And just look at that view!
No wonder people climb up here
every day just to have a look.
Nice people, too. They share their
picnics with me, especially the
children. They feed me bits from
their sandwiches and drips from
their ice-creams. Chocolate ripple
is my favourite.

All summer long, the wind ruffles my fur and the sun is warm on
my back. From up here I can see the fishing-boats sail out
in the early morning sun and come back in the
gold of evening in a cloud of seagulls.
Horrible squawky things, gulls.
Always trying to steal my food.

Then, just as the gulls are settling down and I'm
ready for a bit of shut-eye, that damned dog comes
racing up the hill, barking at everything as usual
before he runs back down to the town.
Barking mad, I call him.

I'm a ship's cat really, but I'm slowly getting used to life ashore. My old skipper and I used to come up to this chapel before we set off on a voyage. He always said a little prayer for fair winds and good weather and then we would walk down the hill to the harbour and sail away into the world.

But my sailing days are over. The ship and the skipper grew old together, too old to sail the seas and too old to look after me.

AUTUMN

It's getting cold up here at night now. Trouble is, the days seem to be getting shorter and the cold nights longer. Not many people climb the hill these days, and those who do don't bring ice-cream.

I still see the boats and the gulls and a few surfers still ride the waves. And I can see an old horse and a donkey playing in a field. Must be nice to have a friend. That yappy dog still races past every day. He barks at everything – gulls, waves, clouds, me.

Every evening I go down into the town to look for something to eat. But I have to watch out. There are lots of town cats around. Rough, tough, greedy cats who chase me off. I usually find some scraps to take home for my supper: a piece of pasty at the back of the bakers, or some dropped chips outside the Take-away. Sometimes the young fisher boy throws me a mackerel when his dad is not looking.

Winter

Brrr. The days are as cold as the nights are now. And wet and windy. When I go out looking for food I get soaked and then can't get dry and can't get warm. Now the horse and the donkey spend most of their time in their stable. I see the man take them out for a trot each day. Then he rubs them dry and gives them a good feed. Lucky beggars!

The weather has been too stormy for the boats to go out so it's been a long time since I had a mackerel. Wet pasty crusts and soggy chips are the best I can hope for. The only good thing is that damned dog doesn't come up here when it's raining.

This evening the little town looks different. There are more stars in the streets than there are in the sky. I can hear singing and I can smell cooking. I think I'll go down and nose around. I'm starving.

The streets are crowded and the shops are open, full of light and colour. I sneak around to the back of the baker's shop. "Hey, you! Beat it! You don't belong round here!"

It's that fat black Tom with his two ginger mates, Rough and Tough. They're big but I'm quick. I race round the corner and in and out of people's legs, down the street to the Take-away.

No good here, either. More cats.
All as striped as tigers and
twice as nasty, tucking into
chips and curry sauce.
People seem to be dropping
more than usual, but the cats
won't share with me – oh no!
They spit at me and
show their teeth.

Next I try my luck at the butcher's
shop but the yappy dog is there.
He yaps at me, and when I run
off he chases after, yapping like a
mad thing, with a string of sausages
round his neck.
Greedy beggar.

I lose him in the crowds and head
up the hill to the safety of 'home'.
I'm tired, hungry and colder
than ever.

Snow has begun to fall.

I try to sleep but I'm too cold.
Then I hear that yappy dog. He's coming up the hill!
He *never* comes at night but I can hear him getting
closer and closer.

Now I can see him through the falling snow, and he's
brought some big mates with him. I don't stand a
chance. I back as far as I can under the steps and my
claws are ready.

Then I see he's got a sausage in his mouth. The sausage smells good.

"Hey, Puss, puss . . ."
It's the fisher boy.

"Come on, your friends are here to see you."

Now I can smell fish.
Lovely *cooked* fish.
The horse, the donkey, the dog and the boy are spreading straw on the snow.

"Come on, Puss. Grub's up."

We sit together in the warm straw and eat. It is a feast, and when I can eat no more I climb into the boy's arms.
He ruffles and strokes my fur.
He is warm on my back.

Bells ding-dong across the bay, and the sea turns silver in the
moonlight. My friends and I sit warm on our hill between
all the stars of Heaven and Earth.